BURN FORTUNE

BRANDI HOMAN

CL◢SH

To those who thought they could charm her wound

For Dan & Scarlett, My Most.
For Jean. For Joan.

It is an heretic that makes the fire,
Not she which burns in't.

SHAKESPEARE

Catch on fire

with enthusiasm

and people will

come for miles

to watch you burn.

CONTENTS

SECTION I: JUNE

I SHOULD TELL YOU

I have a Boyfriend, and it's serious.

I know it's serious because we try to move his stepmother Darlene out of the house, stack drawers filled with clothes in the backseat of My Boyfriend's Cavalier.

It's serious because My Boyfriend's dad comes home and finds us.

You can beat the shit out of me I don't care I'm leaving, Darlene screams.

~

I know it's serious because My Boyfriend gave me Precious Moments. And they are.

I should tell you everyone is afraid of My Boyfriend's dad. When he's gone, we make fun of how he walks tippy-toed, but when he's around, it's different.

~

My Boyfriend's singing voice is so beautiful I cry. He wants to hear me sing too, and I do.

~

I should tell you I'm going to move away with My Boyfriend. I've already bought Tupperware.

SUMMER

We detassel corn for My Boyfriend's dad, the JV wrestling coach. We walk through the fields pulling tassels getting cut and blistered and burnt for five dollars an hour, how I learn what "under the table" means.

My Boyfriend sings to keep me going. He sings "Never Gonna Let You Down," "My Girl," Rick Astley. Songs about how we'll be together forever, how I belong to him.

NAMESAKE

Mother named me after June Carter Cash. Not her voice
—*alley cat twang makes my eyes water,* Mother says—but the
song June wrote that Johnny recorded.

What it should feel like, Mother says, *falling in love.* Her lips
flatten into a line and she pauses before asking if Marci's
coming for dinner.

MARCI V. THE WORLD

Marci makes me join Flag Team. I practice routines with her in the parking lot sometimes just to see what she'll do. She throws her soda at passing cars then flashes her bra *to make the peace*, she says.

She almost hits Kent Burke's Camaro. He mouths the C-word at her, smiles sweetly as he passes. Marci shuts her eyes and twirls.

ARE YOU AFRAID I WILL FLY AWAY

Mother's trying to not show that she's afraid I will actually move away with My Boyfriend. She brings things home after almost every shift at Wal-Mart, an egg poacher, guest towels, a trash can small enough for the bathroom.

Her discount + sale prices = *TOO GOOD TO RESIST*, she says, looking at the inventory in the trunk at the end of my bed. She counts what's there, what's not, remembers the lists in her head, how I know she loves me.

THE CULVERT

Marci and I meet Jeremy outside Centennial Pool. He's a grade older but should be two.

We cross the street to Preservation Park and discover the culvert to the storm drain. The culvert is a round pipe a few feet across that leads to the storm drain's dank cement room.

By *dank cement room*, I mean sewer.

Marci crawls in the culvert behind Jeremy on a dare and lets him feel her up under the new Benetton shirt her daddy brought her from Paris. Her daddy is a bigwig at Russell Tool and Manufacturing, but Marci sucks her first two fingers in public. She twirls her hair so hard it falls out.

Trich-o-trill-o-mania, her doctor says. Marci tells people she has trich.

I sit plucking grass by the entrance to the culvert with my knees tucked under my chin. Nobody's daddy but Marci's is bringing clothes back from Europe. Town stores don't carry Benetton. They do, however, carry cropped t-shirts with neon triangles that look like graffiti, and I want one.

The shirts are 32 dollars.

My folks aren't paying 32 dollars for a t-shirt.

That triangle would lie on me like a stiff, coated tablecloth, Marci's Benetton stripes already bending nicely around the edges.

I holler into the pipe that I'm leaving.

A LESSON

Reaching between the corn leaves, I pull my first tassel. It slides out with a pop, white like a green onion. I drop it to the ground, wet with dew.

The little black insects that were clumped around the base of the tassel are smushed on my palm.

Jeremy says they are spider mites, and spider mites, he says, *crawl up your asshole and lay eggs.*

WHEN THE SEA IS CALM

I have to pee in the field, even though the tape from Corporate Office they play on the first day of the season says not to.

Even though I'm afraid of spider mites in my asshole.

Pulling up my shorts, I hear a rustle, a pounding, but when I stand, the field is empty and the tops of the rows are still.

FLAG TEAM

There's a lot people don't know about twirling flags. I love
practicing with the band in the summer, sweat, horns and
drums too loud to think, the best part. I like the marching,
one-two, one-two. Reassuring, your body knowing what to do.
One-two, one-two. Three four. Like the military but with neon
colors and flashy tricks, dazzle camouflage. My chest tightens
when they're coming, the tricks, my heart like shrink wrap,
but the flag lands in my hands. It always comes down. Like a
sheet for a trampoline in the backyard, I give, hold tight.
Bounce back. Snap to. *One-two. ONE-TWO*.

AMBER

My Boyfriend buys me a ring. It is sterling silver stamped with .925 on the inside to show it's real. My Boyfriend knows this because he bought it at the jewelry store in the mall not the kiosk. There is a leaf on each side of the stone, a leaf with three balls beside it, grapes or something, the silver balls on Christmas cookies that break teeth.

I don't know how he could afford the ring because he can't have a job during the school year, wrestling practice plus lifting and meets.

Maybe he got the money from his grandmother. His grandmother is the type of person who would give you 50 bucks for your birthday after burning your favorite stuffed animal in a barrel out back.

Once we stopped to visit his grandmother. She yelled at My Boyfriend and told him *not to bring any more whores around.*

This is a blood-birthday-money ring.

The stone is amber, which I look up. It's tree sap that's hard-ened, but the best gross thing about amber is the insects, preserved inside it with twigs, seeds, and bubbles for like bazillions of years.

My ring doesn't have an insect, no fly or beetle, but I can see how people would want something like that. Still and whole and kept the same.

My amber has black particles only, flakes. I like to think they're the fly's legs, the beetle's hindquarters. Pieces of claw and tarsus, thorax and antennae.

I like to think my beetle struggled.

I like to think she worked her way out.

BLUTO

The man holding the clipboard on the edge of the field is My Boyfriend's dad. In the rows, we talk about his booming voice, black hair. His tippy-toed walk for height.

He's like that guy in the old Popeye cartoons, what's his name? I say.

Brutus, Chet says.

I don't think that's it.

We wipe the sweat from our brows, sigh.

Bluto, says Jeremy. *It's Bluto, but sometimes they call him Brutus. Copyright or something.*

Bluto's bloated chest, swollen arms.

After this, we call My Boyfriend's dad Bluto behind his back, even My Boyfriend.

DAIRY CREME

The Dairy Creme is an ice cream stand built into the front porch of someone's house. It has two windows and two flavors of ice cream closer to custard but who knows what to call it. An additional flavor is rotated in every few weeks and advertised in block letters in the parking lot with a flashing arrow.

Marci works there before detasseling season. She and her coworker Melanie come up with the most amazing concoctions, chocolate-blue-raspberry slushees, banana-peanut-butter-mint shakes.

For a while, I work at the fast food joint across the street. I am not lying when I say my manager takes fries from one of the trash barrels by the picnic tables, rinses them off, and throws them back in the fryer.

I cannot make this shit up.

Melanie is thrown from the back of a motorcycle and dies. At the funeral, I don't know how to feel because she has been mean to Marci and me but now she is dead and Marci is crying hard enough for both of us so I am embarrassed. I didn't know about open caskets, but there she is, Melanie, an awful orange color, kind of Oompa-Loompa.

I never want to see another dead body again.

GOD HAS CHOSEN YOU AMONG ALL WOMEN

The Gerken Grotto of the Annunciation is this big handmade structure out a little past town. People call it the Jerkin' Grotto and say they're *Goin' to the Grotto* when they mean jerk off. We don't want any pregnancies being announced round here.

The Grotto consists of four rooms plus a shrine. Each room depicts a stage of the Annunciation: The Virgin Mary being startled by the Angel Gabriel, Gabriel telling her she's knocked up by God, Mary questioning the news, and Mary's reluctant acceptance.

Our mayor serves as the president of the board for the Greater Midwestern Grotto Partnership after it was discovered that the Jerkin' Grotto didn't get listed in their annual directory.

I know these things because strangers ask, passing through, visiting relatives, or riding in the Great State Bike Race. They go to the Grotto to ooh and aah over the handiwork—37 years to build—and to admire the semi-precious gems, seashells, petrified wood, marbles, broken glass, coyote bones, and bird skulls planted by some priest and his compatriots a billion years ago.

If you ask me, that priest was bored.

DURANTE

is a fancy Italian restaurant in Pitt Lake. They have candles and cloth napkins and everything.

My Boyfriend picks me up and we drive to Durante.

I want lasagna because I don't know the other dishes—cavatappi, conchiglie, polpettine. After My Boyfriend orders he says *the lady will have* and orders chicken parmesan. They bring our sodas in wine glasses so we toast.

To you, My Boyfriend says.

To us, I say.

We are so romantic. We are having such a good time.

After, we make out in his car in the parking lot.

When My Boyfriend brings me home, Mother flashes the porch lights to say *time's up, come in.*

FLIRTING

Chet and I throw tassels at each other but Jeremy runs at me full force, hoists me over his shoulder.

I kick and scream but he spins and spins, leaves slapping my face like a carwash.

WE ALL HAVE PROBLEMS

But Father is no Bluto.

He shakes my hand when I put it out for money and keeps leftover vanilla-extra-malts in the door of the freezer.

He keeps his glass eye in a mason jar on the bathroom counter when he sleeps, which Marci thinks is gross but is AMAZ-ING. He uses a tiny suction cup to put the eye in and take it out.

Bluto may have broken My Boyfriend's arm but Father would never do something like that, even if he and Mother barely touch.

I bring home a goldfish in a plastic bag that My Boyfriend won flinging frogs at the carnival in the mall parking lot. My Boyfriend and I don't come right home and by the time we do, the goldfish's fins are barely waving.

We sit the bag in the middle of the table and stare, My Boyfriend, Father, and me.

The problem is... My Boyfriend stops, distraught.

Without a sound, Father goes to the kitchen, opens a drawer, and pulls out a straw. He unties the bag, sticks the straw in the water, and blows.

The goldfish's fins start wiggling.

Bluto wouldn't save a spider, let alone a goldfish.

He named the German Shepard Himmler.

GOSSIP

Jeremy tells me the kid a few rows down is from a Small Town Nearby.

He's from the halfway house, Jeremy says.

What'd he do? I say.

Fucked a cow, Jeremy says.

PROOF

Having a boyfriend means someone thinks you're pretty. Mine writes me love poems in pencil on blue-lined paper: my *golden hair*, my *golden heart*. I fold the papers into rectangles, slide them under my pillowcase. The words will smudge but I don't mind.

FARM ANIMALS

We go to the detasseling crew chief Tawny's farm. Tawny has dark hair and canines that jack-knife. She's thirty-something so for all purposes practically dead.

Tawny waves us to the nearest pen. Three cows, pigs, and a goat. I stand between Chet and Jeremy, praying to sweet baby Jesus my tampon doesn't leak.

A goat! Can I ride it? Chet says.

Lord, Chet wants to ride the goat! Tawny throws her head back and spits, thrusts her pelvis.

Everyone laughs. Chet glances sideways and smiles.

Does he want to fuck the goat?

Jeremy had told me about that kid with a cow. *True story,* Jeremy said.

Shit, Chet, you guys want to learn something about riding, stick with me. I know a thing or two, Tawny says.

More pelvic thrusts.

Oh yeah? Chet says.

Shit yeah. Being old means I know how to give it to my husband.

Not one of us wants to picture her giving it to her husband, not ever.

We do things you ain't even heard of. She looks right at me. *I can even do the splits.*

Nuh-uh, Jeremy says.

Oh yeah? Watch. Tawny's shoe slides until her crotch lands on the grass, one arm saluting the air.

Taaa-daah! Bet you boys wanna know how to get someone's ankle like that. She huffs her way upright; I look at my feet.

Now who's thirsty? Patting her ass, Tawny walks toward the house.

SEX ED

My Boyfriend leaves but I stay to check out Tawny's farmhouse. The best thing about it is the kittens, mewing like wildfire in an old detergent box. My tampon slips as I lean over to look. Five or six kittens curl like maggots, grey with white spots, white with grey spots, mostly grey, or mostly white. Tawny's kid appears out of nowhere and hands me a kitten.

They're babies, she says. *I'm gonna have babies someday, too.*

I clutch the kitten and walk into the living room, sitting on the floor in a corner, slapstick crown molding pushing my tailbone. Chet sits beside me in a green chair. He has a buzzed head and stark blue eyes, an eager animal. The chair squeaks as he tilts back and looks around, waiting.

You guys ever seen a triple-X? Tawny says from the doorway, child on her leg. I look up from the kitten. Tawny detaches the kid and strides to a shoebox of VCR tapes.

Jesus, you're kidding. Chet looks at me. Tawny pushes the VCR lid down, presses play.

Two naked people are buttfucking. I'm not sure of the exact mechanics of buttfucking, but I guess this is it. I glance around for the kid, nowhere in sight. Chet groans and covers his mouth. Jeremy laughs. Neither takes their eyes off the screen.

The kitten in my lap is very interesting.

Now that's a different type of pussy. Tawny honks like a trucker. Everyone looks at me.

The cat needs a name, I decide.

Nice pussy, Jeremy says.

Something like Sugar, I think. Rainbow, Sweetpea.

MANNERS

My Boyfriend and I have sex because I love him and that's when everybody says it's ok to do it, but then Bluto makes a joke and puts his hand on my stomach and I know that he knows and I want to die.

I want to die right there.

Take your damn hands off her, I want My Boyfriend to say, but I stand there and feel his dad's hand warm on my stomach. Then I smile because Bluto smiled first.

That's what you do.

Smile back.

PATIENCE

One day, we forget the albino kid from Next Town Over in the field.

At dusk, he walks to a farmhouse nearby, calls his mother.

He says he figured we were still coming.

DINNER DICK

Sometimes Bluto talks about his penis at dinner. *I'd lay pipe to that,* he says.

He burns the burgers and the potato salad comes in styrofoam with a plastic lid. He tears into an ear of corn, snorts, and says, *I'd give her all I got.*

CEREMONY

Mother asks whether My Boyfriend and I will get married.

I hope you don't want my wedding dress, she says.

I rented it for twenty-six dollars.

WRESTLING

Everyone hangs out at My Boyfriend's house when the work day is done. Bluto gets bored and makes us do things. He tells you to do something and calls you names until you do it, unless you're a girl, and that depends on the girl.

But if you're a boy he lifts his baseball hat by the bill and wipes the sweat ring from his forehead with the heel of the same hand, calls you a name. He settles the hat back on his head.

One day Jeremy says My Boyfriend wouldn't know which hole to put it in if he could find it. Bluto lifts his hat, swipes.

You gonna let him call you pussy, Pussy?

Pussy is Bluto's favorite word.

My Boyfriend's head and shoulders curl. He stands, hitches up his pants and lumbers over to Jeremy, locking horns like elk, like he's been taught all his life.

My Boyfriend has cauliflower ear in the off-season.

My Boyfriend wrestles so good he makes other boys cry. They try and hide it but My Boyfriend knows and I know too.

I like this about My Boyfriend, their crying.

What do I burn for?

DREA DELL

A new kid shows up the last week of the detasseling season. Not just any new kid, either.

Drea Dell is a freak.

During band practice, Drea Dell aims the spit from her trombone at your feet. Her nose leaks too so she wears a navy bandana like a dog. Her neck every day, that bandana, her initials embroidered in used-to-be-white thread. She's wanted to be called by those initials—Dee Dee—
since birth.

Come lunchtime, Drea Dell eats with us in the midday sun, sitting in dirt at the end of the field.

I'm so fucking sick of bologna, Jeremy says. He picks it from his sandwich and throws the slimy slice to the ground in front of Chet.

I don't want your goddam bologna. Chet nudges it with his sneaker to My Boyfriend.

Fuck you. My Boyfriend picks the slice up at arm's length, flings it away. Soil-encrusted, it lands in front of Marci, who squeals.

Christ guys, Jeremy says. *It's just bologna.* He tosses it straight up and the bologna lands in front of Drea Dell.

Drea Dell looks at the meat on the ground. We look at Drea Dell. She wipes her nose with her bandana and gathers the remnants of her tuna sandwich into a plastic baggie in her lap. She scoots a few feet away from the lunchmeat.

Then, instead of looking at Drea Dell, or even at the grody bologna, we look where Drea Dell had been. In the dirt is a round, rust-colored smudge, six inches across.

It looks like a field kitten was murdered.

Nobody moves. We stare, overheated sandwiches in our hands. After a decade, Jeremy chokes into a laugh. Chet snorts and Marci bursts into giggles.

Drea Dell turns to look, snot down her lip. She looks back at her sandwich, sets it aside. She leans toward the spot.

Drea Dell begins writing. With a flat index finger, Drea Dell writes in her own menstrual blood.

DD, she writes, plus a scraggly, lopsided heart. She rubs her finger in the dirt, wipes it on her overalls. She picks up her sandwich, continues eating.

After, nobody feels much like working.

THE ROUTINE

I'd like to tell you we don't listen, but we do. We do what Bluto tells us.

The crew decides to go to the amusement park at the end of the season. We bring two vans, there are so many of us. The grey van breaks down, so Chet helps Bluto with the engine. A hundred yards down the road, the green van konks out. We haven't been on the highway 10 minutes.

Bluto is red and huffy, swearing at us or the vans or both. He pops the hood and hollers for Chet, who peers at the engine. Bluto wipes the back of his own neck with his hand. Chet does the work while Bluto watches. Then he watches us.

Bluto watches Marci out of the corner of his eye. I'd like to say that he doesn't watch me, but he does. I see him peek at our thighs, Marci's, mine. I play with the seams of my jean shorts, rubbing them between my fingers like the corner of my favorite baby blanket. The blanket had to be reinforced, sewn shut again and again.

Hey Marci, what about that routine you promised us? Bluto says.
Marci had learned a hip-hop routine by watching the music
video she'd recorded over and over. Watch, practice, rewind.
Repeat. She taught me at breaks, lunch, before
flag practice.

Marci and I aren't clean-cut enough to make cheerleader, and
flag team doesn't hold tryouts. Cheerleader rejects, something
to prove, nothing to protect. I can feel Bluto feeling this about
us. Still, we dust the highway off our asses, stand. As we get
ready, Bluto walks to the front of the van. He pulls a wrench
for Chet from under the driver's bucket seat. We giggle and
push each other, waiting. Bluto turns to face us, crosses his
arms over his chest. He grips the wrench.

Marci counts off: *Five-six-seven-eight.*

I gotta tell you, the routine feels good. We dance with passion.
We dance with joy.

Bluto sighs and turns back to the van.

RACES

On the way to the amusement park, we run races in the truck-stop parking lot after Bluto makes fun of the Asian kid for being Asian or having a small penis. The kid's first name is something but his last name is Wang. He covers his mouth when he eats.

My Boyfriend outweighs Wang by like 300 pounds so there is no point in Bluto having them wrestle. Wang takes offense and suggests a race, serious business. Bluto pulls a whistle from his pocket while Wang and My Boyfriend pick a starting line and crouch. Marci grabs a grease-blackened rag from under the passenger's seat for a flag. Bluto points to a faded parking line, the finish.

I stop thinking about the future at all.

Bluto blows his whistle and Marci lowers the flag. Wang is muscular and lithe; My Boyfriend looks like how lawn mowers sound. He throws his whole upper body forward with each stride, veins hardening in his neck, face the bloody pink of steak. His nostrils go wide and panic floods my body because My Boyfriend is losing, My Boyfriend is losing, My Boyfriend lost. Passing the finish line, he stops and puts his hands on his knees, wheezing, sweat dripping in strings like spit. A blood vessel pops in one of his eyes.

Pussy, Wang says.

THE MEAT CLEAVER

Bluto tells the story about My Boyfriend chasing him around
the kitchen table with a butcher's knife like it's
a joke.

My Boyfriend was seven.

*Aww, what you gonna do this time, little girl? You gonna chase me
around the table with a meat cleaver?*

Bluto puts out his lower lip, makes it waver.

Boo-hooooo!

He catches the eye of whoever stands closest and winks, and
the kid, whoever it is, winks too.

I always wink back.

UNDERWHERE

Somewhere outside the amusement park, we are camping in a cow pasture to save money, sitting in a circle around the fire Bluto made My Boyfriend start.

Chet sits against a tree, watching. Despite this, or because of it, I like Chet. Sometimes, when My Boyfriend is in the other van, I let my head droop onto Chet's shoulder. Sometimes, Chet brushes the bangs out of my eyes.

Shadows flicker over the nylon tents. Music from a boombox, woods dark and chirping. A sky made of stars we can't see in town.

When Bluto steps from his tent, no one notices, but I see Chet's face—not alarm, not yet. Then other faces start changing. Bluto walks the outside of the circle.

He's wearing only a football jersey and tighty-whities.

Jesus, I think, *Jesus*. Then I giggle because Marci is giggling because everyone is. Bluto saunters by, calves glistening, chiseled. He completes the circle.

No one says a word.

Is this a party or what? For fuckssake, turn the music up, Bluto tells My Boyfriend.

My Boyfriend does as told, cranks the dial.

Well don't just stand there with your thumb up your ass, Chet.

Chet's eyes widen and Bluto smiles.

Don't be a pussy. Ask someone to dance.

Chet walks over and offers his hand. As I stand, Bluto steps into the circle next to Marci. The bottom of his jersey runs parallel with the top of Marci's head. She raises her eyebrows. *Wow,* she mouths.

I put my arms around Chet's neck, his skin cool, smooth under my wrists. Hands fumbling at my waist, I hear him mutter.

Shit, he says, *shit.*

I'm going to have to stay up all night.

SECTION II: JEAN / JOAN

THE MERE ICONOGRAPHY DOES
NOT MATTER

In the new high school auditorium, they've hung movie posters from like the seventies that no one cares about. Horrible-sounding movies lined up in a parade above the lobby windows all featuring the same actress. Sometimes I stare at them while practicing flags and pretending to listen to Marci. Sometimes I'm so bored I put them in alphabetical order:

Airport / Breathless / Lilith

Paint Your Wagon / Saint Joan

At least that *Breathless* one sounds okay.

I bet there's sex, lots.

JEAN SEBERG

I start asking if anyone knows the actress in the auditorium posters. Marci doesn't. My Boyfriend doesn't.

I ask flag team sponsor Coach T, who says Jean was from here and got kind of famous but mostly in France, no big deal. She thought she'd seen some of Jean's movies, Jean was decent.

Airport, maybe. *The Mouse That Roared.*

Tell me more about this mouse, I say.

Metaphor, she says.

PAINT YOUR WAGON

Paint Your Wagon is the only Jean Seberg movie the library has. The librarian, Mrs. Devereux, brings me her own copy of Jean's biography from home, says she'll order more films.

This movie's about some miners going west to look for gold. In the opening credits it's all scruffy-looking men. It hits me that I know the theme song, we sang it for chorus in fourth grade:

Where am I goin' / I don't know / Where am I headin' I ain't certain / All that I know is I am on my way

Whoa, there are no women in the *whole town* and when Jean comes to visit, her husband (who already has another wife, Mormons) AUCTIONS HER OFF.

The man who wins is a falling-down drunk who has Clint Eastwood argue for him. No wonder people love Clint Eastwood! I didn't know he ever looked like that, pinched but not the shrunken head he is now.

Oh my god Clint Eastwood is SINGING.

Of course Jean falls in love with Clint instead of his scurvy friend she was forced to marry.

WHAT OH MY GOD SHE MARRIES HIM TOO.

SHE MARRIES CLINT. She has two husbands!

We sang the theme song for two husbands in fourth grade!

And they say the word horny! Several times!

This is one fucked-up movie.

At the end, the whole city falls to the ground.

MAPS

After that weird polygamy mining musical, Jean Seberg has my attention.

How do you start *from here* and end up *there?*

Born and raised.

LUCK

The biography Devereux gives me says the director picked Jean out of 18,000 hopefuls to play Joan of Arc in his movie *Saint Joan.*

I can't get picked first of twenty for dodgeball.

I can twirl a flag like a motherfucker, though.

Ask anyone.

JEAN, WHY DON'T YOU COME BACK
TO US FOR AWHILE?

After being picked for *Saint Joan*, Jean rode on the back of a convertible in a borrowed mink coat. She was given:

- An orchid corsage
- A key to the city
- A small gold-plated ear of corn.
- A parade, our high school band.

It's the ear of corn that kills me, not quite gold but gold enough. She took it with her to film in England.

It must've felt comforting in her hand, moist on metal. The right size for a purse or pocket. Good to grip, a rock in the fist.

BREATHLESS

Because this movie is not only from a billion years ago but also from France, Devereaux tells me the words appear in English at the bottom of the screen.

The first words are *After all, I'm an asshole.*

I've never seen a foreign movie. I watch in the basement with the lights off, curtains closed, a whole bag of licorice fancier than popcorn. I tell Mother to stay upstairs because I'm studying.

A BOUT DE SOUFFLE

This guy looks like an idiot, holding his cigarette in his mouth like that. A pervy idiot looking at high school girls on the side of the road.

Nothing like sunshine.

He points his gun at his reflection in the mirror. The camera's all blurry and I'm kind of dizzy.

He kills a man and runs across a field?

To DRAMATIC MUSIC.

Jazz hands!

I'm bored already.

Does he have herpes? He keeps rubbing his lip.

He steals her money while watching her take her clothes off. Kind of like how Marci used to go upstairs and dance behind the screen during teen night at the club on the edge of town called The Boxx. Everyone knew who was taking her clothes off. Everyone was watching.

Here's Jean, finally. She's so beautiful like movie stars are beautiful.

She does kind of look like an elf, though. She reminds me of that creepy dude who has mushrooms painted all over the roof of his house, gnomes in his front yard. But elf dude's face looks hard.

Why don't you wear a bra? Her costar asks, pokes Jean in the boob.

Live dangerously until the end! He crosses himself and walks away.

The camera keeps spinning. I'm dizzy and their ties are terrible. If he does that thing with his lip again I'll just die. That's the worst fake karate chop I've ever seen.

What? He just *asks* her to sleep with him? Says it out loud on the sidewalk in front of God and everyone? Just like that?

Why are you so mean? He asks.

Why are you so sad? She says.

If I could dig a hold to hide in, Jean says, *I would*. She kisses the new guy but doesn't move her head. The lights come on all at once.

Jean looks at herself in the store widow, pats her tummy. Is she supposed to think she's fat?

He's waiting for her naked in her own bed.

She brushes her eyebrow with a hairbrush. He talks to himself in the mirror, hides his head under the sheet. She holds a teddy bear.

Give me a smile, he says. *If by eight you haven't smiled, I'll strangle you.*

I'm pregnant, Michel, she says, washing her feet in the toilet. Of course she is. She's wearing stripes like a convict. She wants to go to Mexico and the siren is so loud. She has a bruise underneath her fingernail when she smokes.

Take off your top, he says. *Take off your top*. It feels like how when Kent Burke tells Marci to show him her tits. He says it again and again.

Jean looks like she never believes herself when she smiles.

I will never forgive her for that.

Smiling when he says so.

FATHER COMES IN

To watch the news; Mother is watching her show upstairs. I have to stop the tape.

I wait too long to finish and have to take the tape back to Devereux or I'll get a fine. I don't tell her I didn't watch the whole movie even though she asks.

THE PRESENT

I get a camera for my sixteenth birthday *because we already have a car*, Mother says. With her employee discount she could afford it, saved up special. She doesn't say, but I know it's just from her.

I don't know what to take pictures of so I take it to Fisher River Park on the north side of town where My Boyfriend and I go to make out. He never takes his letter jacket off. I make him stand on the bank of the river because rivers are deep.

During a break in flag team practice, I ask Coach T what she thinks I should photograph.

Your life, she says.

My life? I think. *My life is boring.*

BONJOUR TRISTESSE

Hello Sadness is the name of the movie Devereaux gives me next—I know from French class.

There's a marriage proposal in the first two minutes. At least Jean's driving the car—Father never lets Mother drive.

Man, that is a DRESS. Even old-fashioned, that dress is something.

Jean looks creepy looking over his shoulder.

He's pulling her head back by her hair and they're wearing matching outfits.

WHAT IS WRONG WITH THESE PEOPLE. Jean kisses her dad in public more than I kiss My Boyfriend.

I know women. I know how to make them like it, her dad says.

Jean laughs so, so hard.

The only time I've ever been in a conga line like that was at teen night at The Boxx. The song was called DA BUTT.

Her hat looks like a volcano.

Subtle, the bed in the background.

I like Jean so much better when she gets crazy.

Seventeen and drinking. My Boyfriend would never approve.

Their car's as big as our house.

Dammit, there's a crash.

Somebody dies.

SORCERY

I choose *St. Joan* next, even though Joan of Arc seems cliché, a woman wearing clothing for men, woo-hoo.

But everyone loves a witch.

SAINT JOAN

The opening credits are fuzzy balls that swing and dangle. Then the image from the video box—broken soldier, broken sword.

A beautiful castle reversed in a lake, a turreted tower pointing down.

A crown on cloth like a crown is the goal. Lines like electrode rays shooting from it screaming WE HAVE ALL THE POWER.

BRIBERY

Apparently the man who directed *Saint Joan* was a real dick but then he'd buy Jean shit to make up for it, expensive dresses and dinners, a typewriter because she secretly wanted to be a writer.

You're not thinking the part! You're not thinking the part! He'd say.

He'd rub her head, call her baby.

I don't like the way you talk, walk, or dress.

Jean tap-danced in response, wearing 28 pounds of armor.

I tap-danced in the outfield playing softball once.

The man in charge didn't like it when I did either.

YOU MUST NOT TALK TO ME ABOUT
MY VOICES

This must be a flashback because Jean-Joan has long hair, barefoot in a peasant dress. Trying to look determined, crazed, destined. Nostrils lowered, jaw forward.

I hear voices telling me what to do, Jean-Joan says to the man who just dangled another man over the well, a real one, not for wishing.

JEAN-JOAN PASSES THE HANGED MAN

It is an old saying that he who tells too much truth is sure to be hanged.

The man here has black eyes, a warning. I didn't know eyes could go black like that when you die.

It seems right, everyone looking but not seeing, seeing but not saying, saying but not hearing, hearing but not listening, infinity, infinity.

Jean-Joan crosses the man with her sword, rides on.

PICASSO

The director also gave Jean a print of *Child with White Dove* by Picasso, her favorite. Devereaux helps me look it up but it's just *Child with Dove*, nothing white about it.

Have you seen this painting, it's frightening. Child is obviously a girl because there's a big dress, even bigger bow. She has the same haircut Jean-Joan has in *Saint Joan*.

You can't tell whether she's setting the dove free or strangling it.

THE ONLY WORDS SPOKEN
BY ANOTHER WOMAN
THE WHOLE MOVIE

JEAN-JOAN NOT MARVELOUS ENOUGH FOR US

There is always danger, she says.

SECTION III: JUNE

THE LOOP

I'm in Marci's Skylark or My Boyfriend's Cavalier or the Nova Great-Grandmother gave us. The material glued to the roof has come unglued in spots. It feels like felt puppets when Marci or My Boyfriend or I drive too fast and we reach up to steady ourselves. The car smells musty, or like leftover fast food. It smells like My Boyfriend's Eternity cologne or the warm night wind or Marci's hairspray. That she bought at the salon. It smells like Sun-In and Gatorade. It smells like gasoline from filling up at the Kum-n-Go, fumes lingering on Marci's miniskirt she got at the outlets.

Ahead, the taillights of other cars line up to scoop the loop. The streetlights flash off the windshield, each other's jewelry, each other's teeth. The lights blur past in streaks.

I'm desperately trying to get the attention of the boys in the next car by desperately acting like I'm not trying to. I am desperately trying to get their attention by looking straight ahead while driving and hoping they will notice me not noticing or I am desperately trying to get their attention by commenting loudly about the boys in the car *behind* their car or I am trying to get their attention by laughing too loud and Marci's quick, she joins in.

We are fucking hilarious. We are having such a good time.

Or My Boyfriend is driving the car with me in the front seat and Marci and The New Girl in the back and I am trying to act like I'm not jealous of Marci and The New Girl desperately trying to get the attention of the boys next to us. The New Girl leans out the back window and starts to lift her shirt. She is desperate but not desperate enough. Marci is though so she lifts her shirt and the boys' car swerves and everybody screams and My Boyfriend floors it but can only go 20 feet before rear-ending the car in front of us so he slams on the brakes and everybody shrieks and it is epic.

Or I am driving because My Boyfriend is tired because I need the practice because I like to drive. My Boyfriend is riding shotgun. My Boyfriend is a big boy but his teammates in back are bigger and dumber. They are wearing different-colored letter jackets than the boys in the car next to us from Small Town Nearby. Ours are red and black. Theirs are blue and white. We are the Cardinals and they are the Bluejays or Dragons or Warriors. One of their boys spits his chew a little too close to the hand of one of our boys. Our boy says shit or fuck or damn. Their boy says shit or fuck or damn back. Our boy hucks ice from his cup. I yell *EVERYONE BE QUIET* because I can't concentrate on driving and their boy yells *WHY DON'T YOU TELL YOUR BITCH TO SHUT UP* and My Boyfriend almost falls out of the car trying to get to their boys.

We are at the end of the drag but their boys won't let us turn the corner and I don't know what to do. My Boyfriend shouts *just drive* and I am scared because I've never heard him yell before.

Or I've heard him yell but he reminds me of his dad so I
gun it.

TWIRLING

When my parents can't speak and Father leaves before dinner, I take my flag to the dead end of our street. The cement crumbles into field. I don't bother to practice with music; I don't stop when the sun goes down. The mosquitoes swirl in the streetlight as I toss my flag up and spin, over and over and over.

MY BOYFRIEND STARTS
RUNNING AWAY

We find him at the water tower, the lake, behind the dumpster at the Kum-N-Go on Sixth Street.

Car parked on the train tracks, engine still running.

THE CAMARO

The next time Kent Burke drives past us practicing in the parking lot, Marci doesn't try to hit the Camaro with her flag. Still, Kent Burke flips a bitch, drives back round and pulls up.

'Sup, *slut*, he says to Marci.

Marci never takes offense when people call her that. *Freedom*, she says, after going down on a boy from Next Town Over in the men's restroom of the Blue Moon Cafe.

'Sup. She finishes her Hip Turn and walks toward the car, flag trailing like Linus's blanket in the Peanuts' Halloween special.

It's the Great Pumpkin, Charlie Brown!

Marci hooks her elbows over the car door, leans in. The practice tape of the band playing "Smoke on the Water" blares. I ignore them and twirl.

Kent Burke ignores Marci and watches.

Girl, why do you hate? Kent Burke is talking to me now. I blush, keep twirling.

Kent Burke talks to Marci without looking at her. *Why don't you tell your deaf friend to get in?*

I clench my teeth and finish my flag trick. To my own surprise, I walk around the Camaro, chuck my flag in the back seat, climb in.

Drive, I say.

IN THIS DREAM

I am wearing a wedding dress, the one I've been picturing since fifth grade, off-the-shoulder and the like.

Then my nose starts to bleed.

THE BONFIRE

My Boyfriend's house out in the sticks, blanket of stars. The only kid taller than the flames, so thin we call him Twig, bends to put his hands on the ground, fingertips like a sprinter in the blocks. He blows and the edges of the fire go blue then clear. The afterimage of the flames sets black and translucent against the inside of my eyes. I am terrified but suddenly alive. The fire swirls and spits over me, cracks above my head.

LITTLE LEAGUE

Darlene calls to tell me My Boyfriend left crying in the middle of wrestling practice and never came back. From locker room talk, Bluto thinks he is headed to Small Town Nearby, and Darlene is on her way to take me.

If he's coming home for anyone, she says, *it's you.*

Fucking prick, she says, hanging up.

I know who she means.

Darlene uses her time with a captive audience well. She buys me a Big Gulp and doesn't stop talking. Bluto she could fucking leave. He falls asleep to *Star Trek*, weighs My Boyfriend before breakfast. Locked My Boyfriend in the weight room once; the equipment room, twice. Hides My Boyfriend's homework if he doesn't make weight. Stores food under their bed, in the file cabinet, in his car if he has to.

When My Boyfriend was ten, Bluto duct-taped My Boyfriend's feet to the pedals of the exercise bike in the basement.

We find My Boyfriend in the bleachers of the Little League diamonds to the west of town. He sits on his hands in the dark, letter jacket sleeves stiff. His breath gives him away in white shadows, right leg a jittering band saw. He looks small, half his size.

I don't want to go anywhere near him.

Bluto says My Boyfriend is lucky he has a father so disciplined.

Just think, Bluto says, *how good I could've been with a father like that.*

THE NEW GIRL

You know The New Girl is a Satanist, she's been to rehab and it's not even Senior Year.

You know I slide my hands down My Boyfriend's arms and there are moles there. You know I lost the promise ring the day after. You know My Boyfriend and I argue whether it is spelled come or cum. You know I still don't know.

You know The New Girl returns Christmas presents for drugs. She digs butts out of the backseat and smokes them.

You know I get My Boyfriend's book in Biology, where he had written his name on the line the year before. You know I think this is a sign. You know he snuck into my room and put his class ring on my dresser. I tie it with red yarn to fit. You know the yarn matches the stone.

You know. I take the ribbon out of every cassette he ever gave me.

THINGS FALL APART

I mean, Marci's my friend, but she lies. How much hair clips cost, her satin pajamas. Trips she's been on, richer relatives. She laughs too loud, someone always turning to look. She laughs at The New Girl's hair while we eat cookie dough in the kitchen. Marci falls off her stool.

I see My Boyfriend talking to himself in the mirror more than once. He only won the last meet because his opponent got disqualified for throwing headgear on the mat.

I watch him through the crack in the door.

You're fat so fat, he says to the mirror.

He slaps his right cheek, then his left.

DOGMA

I think, deep down, Bluto really does love My Boyfriend.

That's what being a good American is, right?

Be better! Be better all the time!

SAD EXCUSE FOR A SON

Our fight about Kent Burke and the Camaro ends with My Boyfriend talking about Bluto on the blacktop of Russell Elementary.

Wet-faced, My Boyfriend's shoulders slump forward, head shaking. I reach to touch his leg.

Don't, he says.

His eyes are shut, forearms crossed in his lap.

Just don't. He rocks his arms side to side, elbows jutting over his jeans.

I reach for him anyway, catch hold.

Don't you'll hurt the baby, he shouts, yanking his arms away.

My Boyfriend never opens his eyes, resumes the rocking.

You'll hurt him, he says.

Palms on the asphalt, I push myself to my feet, My Boyfriend's eyes still shut as he rocks back and forth.

Back and forth.

ATOM BOWL

I go with Marci to see Jeremy and Kent Burke at Atom Bowl. I hate bowling, everyone watching, fingers in a strange place. I try to count the steps each turn, *one-two-three-release, one-two-three-release*, but no rhythm like flag team.

No magic.

Sometimes I sit next to Marci, sometimes Kent Burke. Kent Burke doesn't say a word but leans back, arm across the orange bench, fingers dangling. He knows there's nowhere for me to sit and I don't mind him knowing.

During frame six My Boyfriend comes in and I freeze, everybody freezes. He turns and walks out.

You better go talk to him, Jeremy says.

I don't want to talk.

I am having a nice time.

Marci rolls her eyes. *Just go*, she says.

My Boyfriend gets out of his car when he sees me. I linger on the sidewalk, hugging my chest.

My Boyfriend walks over and swings, hits the parking sign next to my head.

I scream and duck and run back to the bowling alley but can't go in because people will know. I run along the side of the building, overgrown hedges. Tears in my eyes like kaleidoscope glass and it is dark. My shin hits a pipe sticking out from the building.

I fall face first.

My Boyfriend catches up, bends down, is *sorry so sorry*.

Is crying.

I'll never do that again, he says.

I HAVE THIS DREAM

that's worse than the others. I'm twirling my flag, the fight song. I've known it by heart since before I was born, the whole town does. Every football game, every parade. *Go Cardinals you're the best / put the others to the test / blah blah something all the rest / this motherfucking town is hexed.*

AIR BABY

I am wearing red spandex and a sequined headband, twirling a flag in the Homecoming Parade. My once-white pleather boots are yellow and smell like cat piss.

Still, I am having a good time.

Marci turns from the front row to wink and shake her boobs at me. Coach T shoots her a dirty look, but I finish my Helicopter Toss with gusto.

I am thinking of My Boyfriend and Kent Burke's Camaro when our mascot Chuckie the Cardinal grabs my ass. I can hear Chuckie breathing through the mouth screen in the oversized pasteboard head.

Chuckie high-fives some bystanders. Shaking it off, I reach up and untangle my flag.

My one time in the Camaro.

Kent Burke detailed cars three summers for it and you can't make Kent Burke do anything. He loves the Camaro so much I love it too. It smells like old vinyl and pine tree air freshener.

I don't even know how to think about an imaginary baby.

Because I'm grounded and can't see him otherwise, My Boyfriend is at the Homecoming Parade. I see him by the curb, hulking, swollen like a bullfrog. I can't wave so fake-smile his direction, lipstick snagging a tooth.

Then Chuckie honks my left cheek.

Knock it off, I say. What else to do, flag in my hands, marching.

Hey! Hey you. My Boyfriend points at Chuckie, who shakes his giant polystyrene head and beats his chest. Howling, he slaps more high-fives with the crowd.

My Boyfriend starts walking alongside the flag team. I finish my Around-the-World with my heart in my teeth. Marci looks at My Boyfriend then at me. I shake my head. She turns and shrugs.

The third time Chuckie grabs my ass, My Boyfriend's eyes bulge. *Motherfucker, I said quit.* The flag team scrunches their collective necks. Chuckie stops, points at My Boyfriend. He cocks his elbows sideways, lifts a knee in dramatic exit-stage-left fashion, and runs up to goose me one more time.

My Boyfriend rushes him like a horse out the gates. Chuckie scoots between twirlers for protection, and Coach T turns to see the commotion. The band starts playing "Louie Louie," and I begin the routine from habit.

My Boyfriend dodges the spinning flags until Chuckie is trapped. He grabs Chuckie by the collar, punching and punching. The flag team squeals and scatters into groups, frightened cows. Yanking the bird head off, My Boyfriend sends a peal of Chuckie's blood slapping against The New Girls's face. She wails like a tornado.

Break it up, break it up now! Coach T shoves through the girls. Bright hemoglobin petals rain from Chuckie, spattering his jersey. His right eye splits. A crack sounds, nose and cheekbone.

Then, *whack*! Marci takes My Boyfriend out behind the knees with her flag. He stumbles forward into Chuckie. Marci raises her flag over her head and brings it down across My Boyfriend's back, knocking him to the ground. Chuckie wriggles free, darting away through sequined spandex.

Thwap! Flag to neck, another point for Marci.

This time My Boyfriend grabs the flag and shoves it back at Marci, whose grip slips. The flag catches Coach T's wig— alopecia had left her almost bald—and yanks it clean off. The wig dangles, a limp mop. Then Marci panics. She shakes the pole and the wig surges through air, landing in a spectator's blanket.

Coach T clutches her scalp with both hands, fuzzy like a baby ostrich. She bursts into tears. She runs to her wig, clutches it to her chest, stumbles away.

Marci kicks My Boyfriend with her pleather boot. *Mother-fucking asshole cunt dick!* she yells.

My Boyfriend catches my eye but I can't hold it.

We're done, I say, and we are.

THE WRECK

Mud smears across my flag team t-shirt's neon letters, what I imagine a used diaper looks like. I keep touching it trying to figure out how it got there, walking in circles looking at my fingers. Marci had pulled me from the car because she was worried about explosions after the crash.

The voice is close but sounds far. My seat all the way back because I had a nosebleed. I couldn't see the road but knew the curves around Pitt Lake. *You might want to slow down*, I said. *Slow down*, I say, but the voice keeps saying *Sit down, Sit down,* and I don't know the voice or where it is coming from, nowhere, like god.

The telephone pole horizontal in the grass like a tree fallen in the forest to form a bridge across a creek except there is no creek and here is the car, back end folded in half like a taco. The man keeps saying *sit down*.

Thick, twisted steel cables bound together with lock ties drape across the grass where the pole fell. A shower of orange sparks like fireflies. Orange dots floating in daytime.

I sit down. Marci is standing but crying. Sucking her fingers, twirling her hair, bangs pulled off her face, a mock top-knot, big lips tears freckles mouth around her fingers.

No mud on Marci's shirt. A few spots of darkening blood dripping from her forehead. She stops sucking long enough to touch the wound before putting her bloody fingers back in her mouth.

SECTION IV: JEAN / JOAN

I WILL PUT COURAGE INTO YOU

Jean-Joan tells the Dauphin of France in *Saint Joan*.

How do you "put courage" into someone else?

What the hell is a Dauphin?

I can barely get dressed in the morning.

THIS PART I LIKE

I shall dare, dare, and dare again, Jean-Joan says.

Three times for luck.

Three times like a triple-dog dare.

HOBSON'S CHOICE

Devereux tells me Famous Director once said *The history of cinema is boys photographing girls; the history of history is boys burning girls at the stake.*

Sounds awful but the two aren't so far apart, right?

Atrophy or ash.

I DON'T WANT TO BE THOUGHT OF AS A WOMAN

Jean-Joan says what this whole town knows:

To be strong is to be like a man not a woman.

TEN DAYS

The first thing the biography says is about Jean's death, her body not discovered for 10 days, practically at the police station under a pile of leaves, blanket over her, note in hand.

It seems so sad to start someone's life story with her death.

I guess I'm starting there too.

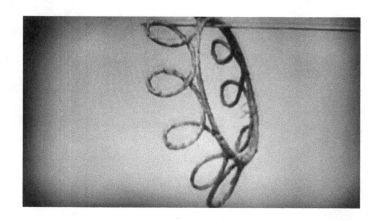

JEAN-JOAN THE ROCK STAR

Storms into the room, cape fluttering and shimmying around her.

A feathered thing, a vision.

Somebody give her the mic already.

THAT CAPE

Really does look like wings. Wings like my hairstyle. Wings like maxipads.

The man in the background looking away.

AIN'T NOBODY

I love watching Jean-Joan because around here the only way to speak is to leave and if you leave you burn.

Ain't nobody rising from the ashes.

Nobody.

THE DAUPHIN

Turns Jean-Joan away after she's served her purpose but this other guy talks about moderation.

He's petting her head like a dog.

WHY WOULD ANYBODY LEAVE

A prison if they could get out? Jean-Joan asks.

Sarcasm, it's called.

Everybody knows you stay.

PICTURES

I dig out my camera to take a photograph of this part, Jean-Joan clutching her head. When the film is developed, you can see my face in the glare from the screen, my hair in color over hers, my fingers around the camera, the picture on the wall behind me that Mother cross-stitched and framed. It's of an antique house filled with antique things, kerosene lamps. The entire house on display, a spinning wheel, each and every thing in each and every room.

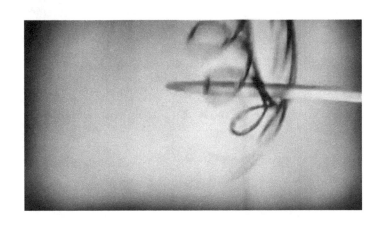

AGAINST YOUR NATURAL
COMPASSION

They lead Jean-Joan into trial and she pauses before a mural on the brick. It is Jesus on the cross and angels.

I bet it's supposed to show that's she's still about Jesus, even now.

Which is witch?

SECTION V: JUNE

NOMENCLATURE

I like to rewind the tapes to the beginning. I watch the movie credits again and try to guess which actor played which character based on their names.

I take pictures of the names I like and save them for future husbands or babies.

Marci likes the name Stephano. I like *Giovannnnnnnnni*.

SWEET DREAMS

I think about My Boyfriend all the time now that we're broken up, how he covered my knees when cold. How he spelled I LUV U in rose petals in the front yard.

The last time I saw him he was sitting in his car at the end of the street because Father wouldn't let him inside. I went to the window every so often.

Still there? Yep.

Still there? Yep.

Then Father went out to say goodnight.

SLEEP

My Boyfriend doesn't drink so when we break up I do, spend the party with my bikini top on backward. Marci has a beer in each hand and one down her shirt for safekeeping.

After most everyone passes out, we find Chet sitting under an umbrella in the bathtub with the shower turned on.

I wake sometime in the middle of the night.

Jeremy stands over me, holding my waist between his feet.

HERE'S THE KING FOR YOU

Our Homecoming King is a fifth-year senior, everything you need to know.

He cries when they put the crown on his head, drape red velvet around his shoulders.

THE TORNADO SIREN

is going off but I don't care. I'm lying down in the flatbed of Jeremy's truck in the high grass by the creek. Jeremy is smoking and impatient to go find Marci. He dangles his cigarette out the window.

Let's get a move on. He cranes his neck to look in the rearview.

A car is the safest place to be in a tornado, I holler, settling my head best I can into the narrow rut of the truck bed, keeping the camera steady, straight to sky, roiling gray and green. Green like money. Green for miles.

I listen to the wind, ditchweed bugs buzzing in frantic circles.

The first drop of rain hits the lens.

NUMBERS

Sometimes Marci and I end up places we've never been. She goes into a bedroom and I make small talk in a kitchen yellow with smoke. Or she goes into the bathroom and I listen to water splash. Sometimes when the water splashes it's ok. Other times, not. The beer tastes like water tastes like beer. The kitchen is beige featuring beige. The couch is navy or forest green or burgundy. These guys are older and their names the same as every boy we've ever met. Boy One is small, pinched. Boy Two is next to me on the couch. I'm tired of beer-water, tuck the can between the back of the couch and the cushion. No, I tuck it into my jacket, hold it tight, a wounded bird. I put my head on Boy Two's shoulder. When I wake, Boy One is laughing. Where is Marci? Boy One laughing and blurry. I widen my eyes, try to sit. Boy Two's hand is in the way. Boy Two's hand is inside my bra, my shirt unbuttoned. Boy One laughs and laughs.

THE SCRATCH TEST

When her dad comes back from a business trip Marci uses a thumbnail to scratch the back of her hand, counting scrapes until she bleeds. *How many licks does it take to get to the Tootsie Roll center of a Tootsie Pop? One? Two?* She rationalizes that this is better than the girls who carve initials into their ankles.

When I get nervous, I scratch my palms with my middle fingers. I hide the rough pink patches so nobody sees.

I do lots of things nobody notices.

THE HAUNTED HOUSE

Jeremy wants to go to the haunted house, the one they used in the tornado disaster movie. *Just the place*, he says.

Chet drives, a beige whale. It's warm and dusty on the upholstery. I sit in back next to a pile of pop bottles, Marci up front on Jeremy's lap holding the roof with one hand, drink in the other. I squeeze my feet next to the case of beer on the floor and look at the glow on Marci's face from the dash.

None of us are beautiful in the pale green. All of us are.

We arrive at the house, stumble out. A few feet ahead, Chet turns and reaches back an open hand. *Come on*, he says. Just like that.

Jeremy and Marci get to the porch first, dropping the beer in the dirt. Chet leans down and paws me one, then one for himself, popping the tops. Never lets go of my hand.

Jeremy throws a flashlight in through the door, ventures

inside a few steps. The light switch doesn't work, enough electricity running through us to light a football field.

We scoot in as our eyes adjust to the dark, silent until Chet pokes Marci's waist and she jumps and I scream. He turns and brings the beer in from outside, cardboard swinging from his fingers.

Marci and I settle cross-legged in a patch of moonlight from the window. Jeremy sits behind her and she leans back. Chet next to me, the beer. Everything
condensing, happy.

It doesn't take long before Jeremy leans down to make out with Marci. I have another beer. Another. And another.

Finally, Chet turns to me, gestures with his head to the rackety stairs.

Come on. Just like that.

IN THIS DREAM

I am twirling a flag, love, it feels so good colors whizzing by, fast as I can imagine I want to go. Red and pink and black lined with silver. I am always in the parade, sequin headband, pleather boots.

In this dream, it starts to snow. The wind whips my face, makes the tears come, fingers hard to move. My toes cramp as the snow begins to drift. My heels slip. I march, twirl, march, twirl, bright comet in midnight sky. The snow piles. I can barely move my legs. Waistband wet, chest heaving, forehead on fire.

I know someone is watching, somewhere, so I keep chin up.

The insides of my cheeks stick to my teeth.

My earrings blister to my ears.

THE EVOLUTIONARY APPETITE

Upstairs, Chet peels my t-shirt up over my arms and I hold them there, genie princess. Let him look. Moving toward him, I stumble. Everyone says sex is such a big deal but it feels good to be out of my head. I lay back on my t-shirt and he lowers himself to me, skin cold, blood hot. My hair catches the floor planks. I want to feel like we own each other but I don't, so I roll back into my skull. Outside is jarring. Inside, coddled with fluid. I slosh and slosh.

.

He pulls my hips, turns me over. I have never done it like this before. Low, I low. *Uhhhhhh. Yeah baby, take it.* Flow and slap. Shadows and swirl and the white line of the windowsill. The rough grains of wood under my hands.

A pause and silence. A sharp, a widening.

My teeth go cold, dry. The wood under my hands. The window.

Hold on. Hold on.

The window, the white, the sill.

Jeremy finishes on my back, wipes himself off.

I flop to my stomach, cheek on fist. Breathe, I breathe.

Apparently Marci didn't want to make out with Jeremy any longer, had walked to the light on the blacktop to pout and wait for a passing car.

I guess you could say I'm not friends with Marci anymore.

FALLING ACTION

There is nothing to do but sit up, get dressed, go downstairs. Halfway down I vomit, splattering my legs and shoes with beige bile.

Chet is outside the house, leaning next to where there used to be a door. His silhouette is blackish-green and he wipes his mouth quick before looking at me. I wipe my mouth with the back of my hand in return, rub it on my jeans.

When I wake I'm in the back of Chet's car. He's draped a thin flannel shirt over my body. We're parked two doors down from my house, away from the streetlight. My mouth tastes like metal and rice.

As I climb out the door, he nods and I nod back.

DIVINATION

Marci tells everyone My Boyfriend used to beat me, moves out of our locker like a divorce.

The New Girl lends me a Magic 8 Ball.

I shake it and am most definitely not pregnant.

I am most definitely not.

I am most definitely.

I am mostly not.

YOUR LITTLE HOUR OF MIRACLES IS OVER

At his party, Chet tells me he wants to talk about Jeremy, so I follow him. The green carpet on the stairs worn to thread. I concentrate on putting my feet in those spots, grey and greasy. Diagrams for dance lessons. I place my palms flat on the walls to either side to keep my balance: palm-palm, step-step. I follow Chet up the stairs.

I don't know if the whisky is good but it works. The New Girl laughing from the family room below. Pictures of Chet along the stairs at misplaced intervals, none of the frames the same. Even when he looks happy he still looks sad. Even before he had whiteheads he looks like he'd have them.

The room, is it his? No posters, no pictures. A clock radio on the desk and a mahogany chair. A graying t-shirt draped over an ironing board in a corner. No sheets on the bed.

I sit on the bed and close my eyes to the room, the grey-brown-white of it. It looks like I feel. Chet shuts the door.

His tongue soft and flat, thick. Different than I remembered. I like the weight of it in my mouth.

He has a stomach where My Boyfriend had none. It rolls out in pinches over the top of his jeans. My fingers flap over the folds, cards stuck in bicycle spokes.

Clothes off, off, skin off. The stitches along the mattress scratch my back. My breast in his mouth. I can no longer feel my hands but still they move.

It isn't that I don't want this it's that what I want is something else and *that* is not *this*. Chatter downstairs, music jagged. My toes are cold and it's dark. A murder of hands, an applause. A mosh pit of hands and holes and wailing and the overhead light flips on. A camera flashes. Laughter from the hallway.

Chet is gone and I do not recognize myself naked under the light. No trophies. Not one poster. I see myself on the table, marked for amputation.

SECTION VI: JEAN / JOAN

UNTITLED

I like the close-ups of Jean-Joan's face the best and use the remote to pause the tape.

I like it when her mouth is open.

It makes me want to scream and scream and scream.

JEAN-JOAN SURROUNDED BY MEN

Men lean over Jean-Joan in clumps, close. Talking at
her face.

I can feel their weight on my chest. I can feel their breath on
my neck.

I can feel their _____ on my _____ .

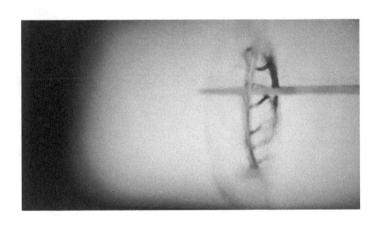

JEAN-JOAN IN CHAINS

In the movie, they tie her at the neck, the chest, the hands.

Her legs are not tied just yet.

Her legs are not bound.

IF YOU ARE A WOMAN THE FLAMES
ARE SEEN AS TOO CLOSE

Jean-Joan holds a makeshift cross, two sticks in front of a huge mound of kindle like those butterscotch cookies made from chow mein.

I can't stand to watch.

The biography says Jean was burned, only one take.

Jean-Joan actually on fire: *We got it all on film,* the director said.

The crowd reaction was fantastic. I'll probably use some of it.

NOT A BONE, NOT A NAIL, NOT A HAIR

Heart.

All of Jean-Joan that's left.

JEAN-JOAN SAYS

She was *born for this.*

ARE YOU ANGRY, JOAN?

Yes.

WHAT DO YOUR VOICES SAY NOW, JOAN?

People await to see you, Joan.

Go home, Joan, go home.

Joan, take back your words.

Have you been hurt, Joan?

Pride will have a fall, Joan.

Cross your legs, girl.

Lie down. Don't be afraid.

Joan, we've given you many hours to think.

How do you know that, woman?

Joan, try to put your trust in us.

You hear, Joan, you have seen the instruments.

Joan, the church instructs you that these visions are from the devil.

Joan, Joan, do you know what you're saying?

Answer, Joan.

We are all trying to help you, Joan.

Do not despair, Joan.

Do you understand this, Joan?

Stay where you are, woman.

Come, child, take the pen.

J-O-A-N. Make your mark.

SECTION VII: JEAN / JOAN / JUNE

THE SHOW MUST GO ON

Marci and I are no longer friends but we still have flag team practice together. I ignore the other girls who ignore me ignoring Marci. When Marci stands too close I smell her hairspray and lipstick, her pink-bottled perfume. I bring my flag down too soon, a half-beat, quarter-note maybe. Marci yelps but I don't stop the routine. Coach T says when we make a mistake to just keep going.

THE INEVITABLE FLATTERIES OF TRAGEDY

I can't sleep most nights so I read. I scoot the stereo next to my bed for its orange glow and use a flashlight to see. A chocolate chip drops onto the book from the cookies I stole from the pantry. It dissolves under my thumb in a thin brown smudge.

The orange light reminds me of when My Boyfriend pulled over onto the side of the road for no reason. I sat on the hood of the car with Marci and watched My Boyfriend and his friends sing in the streetlight, the headlights, translucent halos.

The orange light reminds me of Father driving on vacation. Mother asleep across the backseat and my feet on the dash. A hundred miles from anywhere so Father talks. We talk. After, I lean my forehead against the window, surprised by the cool glass.

I've stopped combing my hair.

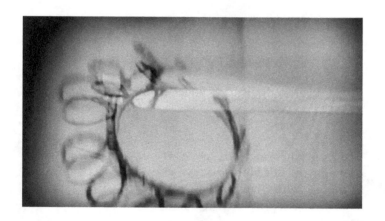

A SHORT HISTORY OF MY
ATHLETIC CAREER

I will never quit flag team, even if Marci and I aren't friends any more. She can cry to Coach T all she wants.

I fucking love flag team.

RECURRING DREAM

When I am able to sleep, I dream about my period. This one a school assembly, the gymnasium. Sitting in the second level of bleachers, hiding in back, I realize they are going to call me down to the gym floor, I've done something. They are going to tell everyone what I've done and then I remember that I have my period and know that I have my period but left my purse in my locker. I don't have time to go to my locker, they are going to say what I did any time now. The blood pools. I try to reassure myself but *is it showing is it showing?* I lean away from the girl next to me, cross and uncross my legs. Blood falling in clumps. They will call me any minute. I crawl over one person and the next. *Excuse me. Excuse me again.* I make it to the end of the row but no longer know where the bathrooms are. *Do you know? Do you?*

THE CLOSET

It's no longer enough to sleep next to the orange glow from the radio. I slide open the closet door, dig out the dirty clothes and beat-up sneakers, enough for a me-sized hole. I climb in, bringing a flashlight and my shoebox of special things—the sand dollar Father gave me, a rock from the mountains, scratch-n-sniff pencils from my fourth-grade boyfriend, and a dog made from stone in Mexico. Three unused cannisters of film and a drawing of a mermaid. Pictures of Mother and a grandmother I never knew, aunts I never see. A note from my second-grade teacher that says she thinks I can do anything, anything at all.

ELVIS

Marci stands next to The New Girl by her locker and when I walk past stops twirling her hair long enough to lean back and honk one boob at me—I mean, tit to chin—keeping the two fingers of her other hand solid in her mouth. Then she curls one side of her upper lip in a snarl like Elvis, shows a few teeth above her wet knuckles.

I imagine her barking. I imagine smacking that fat lip even fatter.

INVINCIBLE

I'm bored and watching TV with Mother when *The Legend of Billie Jean* comes on. I've seen this movie a hundred times —*FAIR IS FAIR*—but when they come to the scene at Lloyd's house I'm startled because the movie they watch before Billie Jean cuts her hair is *Saint Joan*. Lloyd even says it, *Saint Joan*. Jean-Joan talking about lambs crying through frost. Lloyd gives her a camera.

That girl's from here. I slap Mother's shoulder.

Who?

The actress on the movie they're watching. This is her hometown. Her name's Jean, she's from here.

No she's not, Mother says.

THE BIOGRAPHY SAYS

that Joan was *destroyed before fully grown*.

Stripped of potential before knowing to look for it, before looking.

We've been told to behave for so long.

THE LEGEND

At the end of *Billie Jean*, the girls in the movie start cutting their hair off, like Billie Jean cut her hair off in the movie, like Jean cut her hair off in real life, like Jean-Joan cut her hair in the movie, like Joan cut her hair in real life.

The biography says in France, girls would tell hairdressers to *Give me the Jean Seberg.*

Billie Jean looks cool as fuck—reflection shimmering over the pool like an angel, a ghost, the wetsuit she's cut into a vest, her one earring. If fire is coming, she's liquid.

I think about cutting my hair off but like to pretend people can't see me when my hair falls over my face so no dice.

PARACUSIA

The Legend of Billie Jean makes me curious about Joan not just Jean-Joan. Deveraux falls all over herself, sloppy grin like a dog out the car window. She gives me two books and orders more.

The biography says Joan started hearing voices at the "onset of puberty," around 12 or 13. I take this to mean WHEN SHE GOT HER PERIOD. How strange to get your period and have people start talking in your head.

I could have used some voices. When I got my period, I didn't tell anyone. I took a Maxi Pad from the hall closet and went to school. We watched *Old Yeller* while I bled onto the chair. I left class like nothing happened and hid in a mint-green bathroom stall for two hours. At the end of the day, I walked a mile home in stained shorts. I took the back way to my room, would not come out for anyone.

TONIGHT

The shoebox in my closet doesn't work.

I hold it in my lap, turn the flashlight off.

FLOOR DUH LEES

Devereux continues to be so excited I can't say no, let her pile books into my bag. I flip through them and see Joan's crest in color, sword through crown with a fleur-de-lis on either side.

I look at the picture a long time. It looks like the crown is punctured, pierced. The fleurs-de-lis look like corn tassels and that's the god's honest truth.

THE BIOGRAPHY SAYS

that Joan wore men's clothes so she wouldn't be raped.

Imagine. Clothes as repellent, shield.

Doors her companions can't unlock.

WALKING AFTER MIDNIGHT

I start walking at night, sneak out through my bedroom window. It's ground floor and barely locks. I walk until I find a place to crouch, be small. A corner next to a dumpster at the Kum N' Go on Sixth Street. The back of the Dairy Creme. The top of the slide, Russell Elementary. I even walk to the Jerkin' Grotto, this town so small there's only a chain-link fence. I press my hands face mouth through the cold metal, taste it on my tongue. The bazillion surfaces of the Grotto sparkle under tangerine streetlight, spill into dark pockets. I'm an animal and want in.

NOT A MAN WILL FOLLOW YOU

They told Jean-Joan-June.

I shall not look back.

LILITH PART ONE

Mother smokes in the kitchen but when she sees the movie is black and white comes to join me.

Insanity seems a lot less sinister to watch in a man than in a woman, doesn't it?

Mr. Bruce has hair like Elvis, a chin like Travolta. I'm bored but stick with it. The biography says this is Jean's best role. It's an insane asylum for the wealthy. A clock is ticking.

There's Jean, head on the table. *Are we going on a picnic?* She asks.

I'm trying not to think about her hair.

Jean watches the surface of the river sparkle like rhinestones, like asphalt, sequins. She keeps looking at her reflection and laughing. She wears a scarf and sketches in the rain.

Jean has her own language, she says, one *very few people are permitted to speak.*

I'm responsible for you, Mr. Bruce says.

Bruce is Bluto's real name.

The water roars. At this point you want her to jump. At this point, you want to jump.

Warren Beatty, Mother says, *is Mr. Bruce's real name.*

Jean's doctor says schizophrenia can be induced by spiders. They spin asymmetrical webs, *nightmarish designs.*

HIARA PIRLU RESH KAVAWN

That's Jean's own language written on the wall of her room. The ceiling is bowed, caved in, arched.

Even I know Mr. Bruce is talking about sex. *You come here for adventure?*

Even I know the spiders are a metaphor.

Wading in the river, Jean holds her skirt up and kisses her reflection in the mirror.

Next she catches her hair in the loom where she's weaving. WB—what kind of a name is Warren?—pulls the hair out with a scissor blade.

It's almost like she wants to share this magic little world of hers, he says.

How dare she.

Rapture. That's a very good word for it.

Call me Lilith, Jean says. She has dimples and a slight gap in her overbite, just like My Boyfriend.

You've got blood on your face, she says. *You think I infected you?*

Their laughter hurts more than crying.

I'm feeling lonely.

I put the remote under my front teeth, prop my head up to watch. *That was some storm we had last night.*

They're somehow at the County Fair? And there's jousting??

HE BUYS HER A DOLL WITH A CROWN.

My Boyfriend bought me a doll, once; it came in a shoebox with green tissue paper and a dozen roses. He said it reminded him of me. I buried it in the closet. Its dress was blue with white dots and it was wearing an apron.

The crown falls off the doll in the next shot. By the next-next shot, the crown is back on.

WB wants to spear the ring like he used to as a kid. Jean hands him the lance after he mounts, ties her scarf around his arm. *Prepare to charge.* Men always trying to shove things through a ring.

WB wins while wearing sunglasses. They ask him, *Is this your lady?*

They put a wreath on her head, crown her *queen of love and beauty*. There's a wreath in the holiday box under our stairs.

It's killing me that I don't know what the words on her wall mean.

There's montage of her face while she and WB do it, hair in the hay, shiny rhinestone water reflection layered on top. I bet this is supposed to mean something. It looks like sparks, like fireflies.

We know the other girl's dangerous because she's brunette and in shadows.

Jean and the brunette go off into the woods holding hands. We see their faces upside down in a river. He catches them dressing in a barn, slams the door behind him.

You dirty bitch, he says to Jean.

He kisses her and they do it in the hay too.

They all pretend to leave together.

I will never think black and white movies are boring again.

SIDEPLOT

WB's ex-girl is married to Gene Hackman. Mother says Gene Hackman's sexy in an unassuming way. I promise you, I will never think Gene Hackman is sexy, not ever. He looks the same then as he does now.

WB's ex-girl—the one who got away—now can't get away from Gene Hackman. She serves the coffee.

The ex-girl says something like, *Remember when I told you I'd never let you make love to me until I was married? Well, I'm married now.*

Mother crosses her legs, puts out her cigarette.

LILITH PART TWO

WB takes back the doll he bought Jean, drowns it in a fish tank, fins barely waving.

You think they can cure Lilith? Jean asks. *You think they can cure this fire?* She rubs her hands down the outside of her dress. I pull the collar of my shirt up over my nose.

She wants to leave the mark of her desire on every living creature in the world.

I don't kill the things I love, she says. *They jump.*

Jean hides under the covers. *Leave me alone*, she says.

Help me, he says.

Help us, I think.

Help us all.

WHEN I WALK PAST THE LIBRARY NOW

I see Devereaux through the window. She sees me looking and waves. I act like I haven't seen, pull my books closer. Her face falls.

After a while, even The New Girl stops calling. I see her in study hall, her backward baseball hat, gold hoop earrings. She's gotten braces with rubber bands, opens her mouth like a cobra, saliva stretching jaw to jaw. She plucks a rubber band like a banjo and Kent Burke laughs. He takes a tampon from her purse and shoots it across the room.

DO YOU SEE WHAT I MEAN

About the burning?

Joan could have taken back what she said and did. But when faced with prison all her life, Joan gave them the big fuck-you. *I said what I did for fear of the fire.*

Joan chose to burn.

SECTION VIII: JEAN / JOAN / JUNE

CULVERT AS GROTTO

I run out of places to go at night but remember the culvert. I crawl in through the tunnel with my flashlight. It is surprisingly bright inside, light peeling in from the grate.

I leave the shoebox in my closet but bring a few talismans, the shell, stone dog. I steal Father's spray paint from the garage and Mother's nail polish, some glue. Tape. Candles. I've ripped a picture of Jean out of the biography and tape it to the sewer wall opposite from the grate opening, high enough so as not to get wet.

IN THIS DREAM

Father and I are on vacation to like the Grand Canyon though we've never been. From a distance, we watch Mother carry a pink cake—angelfood, I think—straight off a cliff. She is wearing her employee vest with my flag team photo button pinned to it.

We go get her body, Father and I. He can't lift her, so I carry her across my back, my shoulders, her bashed-in face matting against mine.

AND YOU WILL TAKE HER
WORD FOR IT

I start bringing things I find on my walks with me into my dark place in the culvert. A safety pin, playing card, pop tops. An earring without its pair. I mingle them among old photos I've taken, supergluing everything to the cool cement walls above the waterline. A scrapbook of my lives whose smell lingers like rust in the cracks of my fingers.

I tell Mother I need more superglue for an art project at school. I tell her I need red spray paint.

AND I WAS OBEDIENT
IN EVERYTHING

In my culvert, I spray paint stalks of corn, hearts, under the pictures of Jean and Joan, fleurs-de-lis instead of tassels. I spray paint Joan's crest, a sword through a crown. I surround myself with my own garden, hard and flat and smooth. I wipe a red drip with my finger, sign my name on the floor. I use lipstick to give Jean a sword.

STRANGE FIRE

I see Mother talking to a man at church. I notice because Mother doesn't talk to anyone. He looks familiar, Wal-Mart maybe. He is wearing beige and balding and reminds me of Gene Hackman.

THE DAY MOTHER LEAVES

I cut fifth period, walk behind the auditorium to where I usually park. A pastel Post-It is folded in half and tucked under my wiper.

One side reads: *I love you.*

The other: *It burns, burns, burns.*

THE BIOGRAPHY SAYS

That in the? some? most? battles, Joan didn't carry her sword.

She carried a flag.

HISTORY ALWAYS OUT OF DATE

I pick the best picture I can find of Mother and glue it to the wall of my dark place. She's wearing red pants and the most amazing cape I've ever seen—black and white and paisley like playing cards. I remember hiding under the cape in the hall closet when I was little, woven and thick like a blanket. She's looking off in the distance, smile or smirk.

When she left she took the contents of the trunk at the end of my bed, the stuff she bought when I wanted to marry My Boyfriend. Plastic cups, cloth napkins.

Father says she's coming back.

PARTHENOGENESIS

The following day, the test reads positive.

So does the next.

I'm in the Burger King bathroom and decide I can't cry, I won't. I drink all the soda I can through a striped plastic straw.

EVEN I KNOW THIS IS A METAPHOR

The flashlight I bring to the culvert dies so I light a back-up candle Mother kept in her nightstand with self-help books. I drip wax onto the ground, watch it layer over the dirt below like ocean over sand. I use the candle's own wax to anchor it in place.

TO TELL YOU TRUE

Mother's gone and I puked so hopefully Father thinks I'm hungover.

I have to tell him, I think.

I will never tell him, I think.

THINGS SWIRL IN MY MIND

Like a flood all the time. I want My Boyfriend back. I want My Mother.

I'll be better. I'll be better all the time.

LET US PUT GLOWING EMBER
AGAINST GLOWING EMBER

I don't know what an altar is technically supposed to look like because I never paid attention and we stopped going to church when Father could no longer force me into the car.

I think my pictures in the culvert are an altar, a map. I blow on my fingers to keep them warm, then touch each picture, once.

How did she do it? How did *she*?

The pictures look glossy but sometimes my finger still catches.

HIARA PIRLU RESH KAVAWN

HIARA PIRLU RESH KAVAWN

HIARA PIRLU RESH KAVAWN

HIARA PIRLU RESH KAVAWN

HIARA PIRLU RESH KAVAWN

BLESSED BE

I put the candles all around me in a circle but don't know why. I put the plastic Christmas wreath from the holiday box under the stairs on my head. It has crusty fake snow on the tips, tiny pinecones. The candlelight makes me feel warmer somehow but I hug my knees to my chest, put my head on my knees. I watch the light, the shadows, think about Marci, about Mother. My blood pulses, I can feel it. I am sitting still but moving. I am moving. I am moving, still.

WE USED TO LIVE IN THE TOWER

Curled up, I think about that time I ran away from home in seventh grade, hid at the top of the elementary school slide for hours.

Watched Father's headlights as he drove past, back and forth.

Back and forth.

IF YOU AREN'T BUSY I THINK
I'M ON FIRE

The sun cracks through the gutter. The side of my face I slept on doesn't move, like a cavity has been filled. Half of me is numb. The parts where the halves meet tingle, ripple, burn.

MUST I BURN AGAIN

I hold the camera up and turn it toward me, blood inside.

Fuck this place, fuck everything. I look straight into the lens.

Somebody needs to tell.

Anybody.

I put my finger on the button.

Light your fire, I say.

NOTES

Dedication:
Is a play on a line by Willard R. Trask from *Joan of Arc, Self Portrait* (1936).

Epigraph:
Is from *The Winter's Tale*, William Shakespeare, Act II Scene III.

Frontispiece:
Is from a fortune cookie.

Are You Afraid I Will Fly Away:
Title is a line from George Bernard Shaw's *Saint Joan: A Chronicle Play in Six Scenes and an Epilogue* (1924).

God Has Chosen You Among All Women:
Title is a line from Rev. Jesse Lyman Hurlbut, *Hurlbut's Life of Christ for Young and Old* (1915).

Manners:
"Take your damn hands off her" is a line from the film *Back to the Future* (1985).

The Mere Iconography Does Not Matter:
Title is a subtitle in the preface to Shaw's *Saint Joan*.

Paint Your Wagon:
Title is the title of the film *Paint Your Wagon* (1969). Lyrics are from the song "I'm on My Way" by Alan J. Lerner and Frederick Loewe.

Jean, Why Don't You Come Back to Us for Awhile?
Title is a line attributed to a minister in Jean Seberg's hometown in David Richards's *Played Out: The Jean Seberg Story* (1981).

Breathless
The film here is *À bout de souffle* (*Breathless*) directed by Jean-Luc Godard (1960).

Bonjour Tristesse
Bonjour Tristesse (1958), directed by Otto Preminger.

Bribery:
"You're not thinking the part! You're not thinking the part!" and "I don't like the way you talk, walk, or dress" are attributed to Otto Preminger in David Richards's *Played Out: The Jean Seberg Story*.

You Must Not Talk to Me About My Voices:
Title and "I hear voices telling me what to do" are lines from Shaw's *Saint Joan*.

Jean-Joan Passes the Hanged Man:
"It is an old saying that he who tells too much truth is sure to be hanged" is a line from Shaw's *Saint Joan*.

Jean-Joan Not Marvelous Enough for Us:
"[N]ot marvelous enough for us" is a subtitle in the preface to Shaw's *Saint Joan*, and "There is always danger" is taken Shaw's *Saint Joan* as well.

The Camaro:
"It's the Great Pumpkin, Charlie Brown!" is the title of a 1966 animated television special by Charles M. Schulz.

I Will Put Courage Into You:
Title is a line from the film *Saint Joan* (1957).

This Part I Like:
"I shall dare, dare, and dare again" is a line from Shaw's *Saint Joan.*

Hobson's Choice:
"The history of cinema is boys photographing girls; the history of history is boys burning girls at the stake" is attributed to Jean-Luc Godard.

I Don't Want to Be Thought of as a Woman:
Title is a line from the film *Saint Joan* (1957).

Why Would Anybody Leave:
"Why would anybody leave a prison if they could get out?" is a line from Shaw's *Saint Joan.*

Against Your Natural Compassion:
Title is a line from Shaw's *Saint Joan.*

Here's the King for You:
Title is a line from the film *Saint Joan* (1957).

The Evolutionary Appetite:
Title is a subtitle in the preface to Shaw's *Saint Joan.*

Your Little Hour of Miracles Is Over:
Title is a line from Shaw's *Saint Joan.*

If You Are a Woman the Flames Are Seen as Too Close:
Title is a line from Kate Zambreno's *Heroines* (2012).
"We got it all on film […] The crowd reaction was fantastic. I'll probably use some of it" is from David Richards's *Played Out: The Jean Seberg Story.*

Not a Bone, Not a Nail, Not a Hair:
Title is a line from Shaw's *Saint Joan.*

Jean-Joan Says:
"[B]orn for this" is a line from Joan of Arc in *Joan of Arc, Self Portrait*, edited by Willard R. Trask.

Are You Angry, Joan?
Title and "Yes" are lines from Shaw's *Saint Joan*.

What Do Your Voices Say Now, Joan?
This piece is a cento poem consisting of lines from the film *Saint Joan* (1957).

The Inevitable Flatteries of Tragedy:
Title is a subtitle in the preface to Shaw's *Saint Joan*.

Invincible:
"Fair is fair" is a line from the film
The Legend of Billie Jean (1985).
It is also a line from
the film *Saint Joan* (1957).

The Biography Says (that Joan):
"[D]estroyed before fully grown" is a line from Shaw's
Saint Joan.

Walking After Midnight:
Is after the title of a song recorded by Patsy Cline and written by Alan Block and Donn Hecht.

Not a Man Will Follow You:
Title is a line from Shaw's *Saint Joan*.
"I shall not look back" is a line from the film *Saint Joan* (1957).

Lilith Part One, Sideplot, and Lilith Part Two:
Quotations are from the film *Lilith* (1964).

Do You See What I Mean:
"I said what I did for fear of the fire" is a line from Joan of Arc in *Joan of Arc, Self Portrait*, edited by Willard R. Trask.

And You Will Take Her Word for It:

Title is a line from the film *Saint Joan* (1957).

And I Was Obedient in Everything:
is a line from Joan of Arc in *Joan of Arc, Self Portrait*, edited by
Willard R. Trask.

Strange Fire:
Title is probably from something very literary but it is also the
title of a song and album by The Indigo Girls.

The Day Mother Leaves:
"It burns, burns, burns" is a lyric from the song "The Ring of
Fire," written by June Carter and Merle Kilgore.

History Always Out of Date:
Title is a subtitle in the preface to Shaw's *Saint Joan*.

To Tell You True:
Title is a line attributed to Joan of Arc in Mary Gordon's *Joan
of Arc* (2000).

Let Us Put Glowing Ember Against Glowing Ember:
Title is a line from Gaston Bachelard's *The Psychoanalysis of
Fire* (1987).

Hiara Pirlu Resh Kavawn:
Title and text are from the film *Lilith* (1964).

We Used to Live in the Tower:
Title plays off the title of Shirley Jackson's novel, *We Have
Always Lived in the Castle*.

If You Aren't Busy I Think I'm on Fire:
Title is the title of a poem by Wendy Xu.

Must I Burn Again:
Title is a line from Shaw's *Saint Joan*.
"Light your fire" is a line from the film *Saint Joan* (1957).

Biographical information about Jean Seberg and Joan of Arc was informed by the following texts:

Barstow, Anne L. *Joan of Arc: Heretic, Mystic, Shaman*. Lewiston: E. Mellen Press, 1986.
Castor, Helen. *Joan of Arc: A History*. New York: Harper, 2015.
Gordon, Mary. *Joan of Arc*. New York: Lipper/Viking, 2000.
Joan of Arc, and Willard R. Trask. *Joan of Arc, Self Portrait*. New York: Stackpole Sons, 1936.
"Joan of Arc." *Catholic Online*. http://www.catholic.org/saints/saint.php?saint_id=295
McGee, Garry. *Jean Seberg: Breathless*. Albany, Ga: BearManor Media, 2008.
Pernoud, Régine, and Marie-Véronique Clin. *Joan of Arc: Her Story*. London: Phoenix, 2000.
Richards, David. *Played Out: The Jean Seberg Story*. New York: Random House, 1981.
Sackville-West, V. *Saint Joan of Arc: Born January 6th, 1412, Burned As a Heretic, May 30th, 1431, Canonised As a Saint, May 16th, 1920*. Garden City, NY: Doubleday, Doran & Co, 1936.
Shaw, Bernard. *Saint Joan: A Chronicle Play in Six Scenes and an Epilogue*. London: Penguin Books, 2001.

Photographs:
Are from the author's personal collection.

Acknowledgments:
"My spirit was called here by yours" is a line from the film *Saint Joan* (1957).

ACKNOWLEDGMENTS

Sections of this work have appeared in various forms in the following publications. Many thanks to their editors: *Bodega, Booth, The Collapsar, Dream Pop Journal, Grimoire, Requited,* and *tenderness lit.*

Thanks and eternal gratitude:

To Selah Saterstrom, who midwifed the hell out of this book. *My spirit was called here by yours.*

To Laird Hunt for magic words and grace under pressure. To Teresa Carmody and Becca Klaver for love and clarity when direly needed. To the University of Denver for time and support, and especially to Brian Kiteley, Tayana Hardin, Jennifer Pap, Emily Culliton, Mildred Barya, Nancy Thurman, Aditi Machado, Mairead Case, Angela Buck, Lindsey Drager, Vincent Carafano, Sarah Boyer, Eleanor McNees, Donna Beth Ellard, and Karla Heeps for encouragement and assistance. To Corri Golden, Stephanie Manuzak, and the Chicago, Denver, and Buenos Aires writing groups for early, early eyes.

To Julia Madsen, soul sister of corn gothic and Mountain Dew. To Dani Rado and the Denver Bicycle Café for Writing Fridays. To Jenrow. To the editors who've published my work, ever—you make a difference in the world. To Leza Cantoral and Christoph Paul, Queen and King of the New Hampshire hustle—bless you for believing. To Matthew Revert, Steven Dunn, and Mona Awad in adoration. To my magnetic fields Jessi and Kristen.

To my family—Dan, Scarlett, Mom, Dad, Angie, Mom and Dad Singer, and Magoo (R.I.P. Sweet Puppy)—for the love. I love you back.

Finally, to Mrs. Ketchum. Thanks for the note.

ABOUT THE AUTHOR

Brandi Homan holds a PhD in English, Creative Writing (Fiction), from the University of Denver and an MFA in Poetry from Columbia College Chicago. She is the author of two books of poetry, *Hard Reds* (2008) and *Bobcat Country* (2010), from Shearsman Books. With her husband and daughter, she lives in the suburbs of Denver, where she thinks about the Midwest and misses drinking Yellow no. 5.

ALSO BY CLASH BOOKS

WE PUT THE LIT IN LITERARY

clash

BOOKS

FOLLOW US ON TWITTER, IG & FB

@clashbooks